INJUSTICE GANG
AND THE
DEADLY NIGHTSHADE

BY
DEREK FRIDOLFS

ILLUSTRATED BY
TIM LEVINS

⟨ STONE ARCH BOOKS ⟩
a capstone imprint

Published by Stone Arch Books in 2017
A Capstone Imprint
1710 Roe Crest Drive
North Mankato, Minnesota 56003
www.mycapstone.com

STAR38571

Cataloging-in-Publication Data is available
at the Library of Congress website.
ISBN: 978-1-4965-5158-0 (library binding)
ISBN: 978-1-4965-5166-5 (paperback)
ISBN: 978-1-4965-5171-9 (eBook PDF)

Summary: While thwarting an Injustice Gang heist, Batman
accidentally destroys The Shade's cane. As a veil of darkness
blankets the world, the Justice League enacts a bold plan to prevent
a global ice age. Can the world's greatest team of super heroes
reset time to bring light back to the world? Or will the Injustice
Gang gain the upper hand on a planet that's seen its last sunrise?

Editor: Christopher Harbo
Designer: Bob Lentz

Printed in the United States of America.
062017 010598R

CONTENTS

When the champions of Earth came together to battle a threat too big for a single hero, they realized the value of strength in numbers. Together they formed an unstoppable team, dedicated to defending the planet from the forces of evil. They are the . . .

{ ROLL CALL }

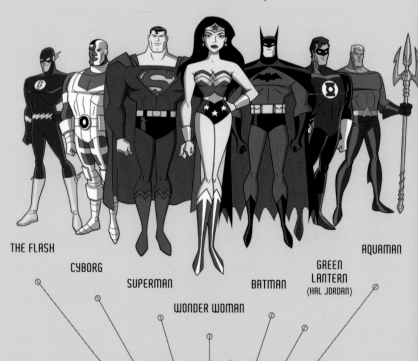

THE FLASH

CYBORG

SUPERMAN

WONDER WOMAN

BATMAN

GREEN
LANTERN
(HAL JORDAN)

AQUAMAN

MARTIAN
MANHUNTER

HAWKGIRL

HAWKMAN

GREEN ARROW

BLACK CANARY

GREEN LANTERN
(JOHN STEWART)

THE ATOM

SUPERGIRL

RED TORNADO

POWER GIRL

SHAZAM

PLASTIC MAN

BOOSTER GOLD

BLUE BEETLE

ZATANNA

VIXEN

METAMORPHO

ETRIGAN
THE DEMON

FIRESTORM

HUNTRESS

CHAPTER 1

GOLD STANDARD

On a beautiful, sunny day in Metropolis, everyone wanted to be outside. Children and pets played in the grass under a cloudless sky. Adults ate their lunches on park benches, enjoying pleasant conversations. Shoppers casually strolled the city's bustling sidewalks, gazing through store windows filled with the latest fashions.

A well-dressed man and his wife gazed into the window of Steffany's jewelry store. The man pointed at the sparkling diamond necklace worn by the mannequin. His wife smiled at the choice.

"You should stick with gold," said a deep voice behind them. "It'll soon be worth more than those diamonds."

The couple turned to see who had spoken, but they only saw a door slam shut on a black stretch limo. The car pulled away, heading down Sixth Avenue.

Using side streets to avoid busy midday traffic, the limo soon arrived in front of a high-rise building. Aside from LexCorp and the Daily Planet Building, this concrete skyscraper was one of the tallest and most secure in Metropolis. It also catered to a very select client.

The limo driver walked to the back of the vehicle. Dressed all in black, he wore a top hat and reflective round sunglasses. He also carried a black walking cane. Only his skin looked pale against his dark clothing.

When the driver opened the back door, a set of leather shoes touched the sidewalk first. Then the passenger's broad chest came forth wearing a finely tailored double-breasted suit. His diamond cufflinks sparkled and his familiar bald head gleamed in the sunlight.

Billionaire Lex Luthor had arrived. As he walked toward the building's entrance, the doors opened to accept him.

"Mister Luthor!" said a man, rushing forward to greet him. "Welcome to the Metropolis Federal Gold Reserve Bank! To what do we owe the honor — ?"

"Business," replied Lex, interrupting the bank manager. "Always business."

Lex brushed past him, walking toward the back of the bank. Luthor's driver followed along quietly. The bank manager jogged to keep up.

"Are . . . are you here to open a new account?" asked the bank manager nervously.

Lex stopped. He scowled at the manager. "In a manner of speaking. Now show me to your vault," ordered Lex.

Flanked by multiple guards, the manager led Lex and his driver down a long hallway. At the end of it stood a round steel door with a wheel. All along the hallway, video cameras peered down from the ceiling. Motion sensors lined the floor. The bank's security system even included 24-hour satellite monitoring technology. All in all, the vault had enough security to protect the 100,000 gold bars it held in reserve.

"How much do you wish to deposit?" asked the manager, rubbing his hands together.

"Them," said Lex, motioning behind him.

With a tip of his hat, Lex's driver stepped forward. He raised his walking cane and waved his hand. A black teleportation portal opened out of thin air.

Cheetah, a feline criminal with spotted fur and sharp claws, emerged from The Shade's portal first. She landed on all fours as a purple glow followed her out of the darkness. That light, cast by a crystal stone in her mask, carried Star Sapphire. She was an enemy of the Green Lantern Corps who took on any job if it meant she'd get rich.

Close behind Star Sapphire came Solomon Grundy and the Ultra-Humanite. One was a soulless zombie whose torn clothing barely hid his huge, pale frame. The other was a mutated albino gorilla whose oversized forehead held a vast intellect.

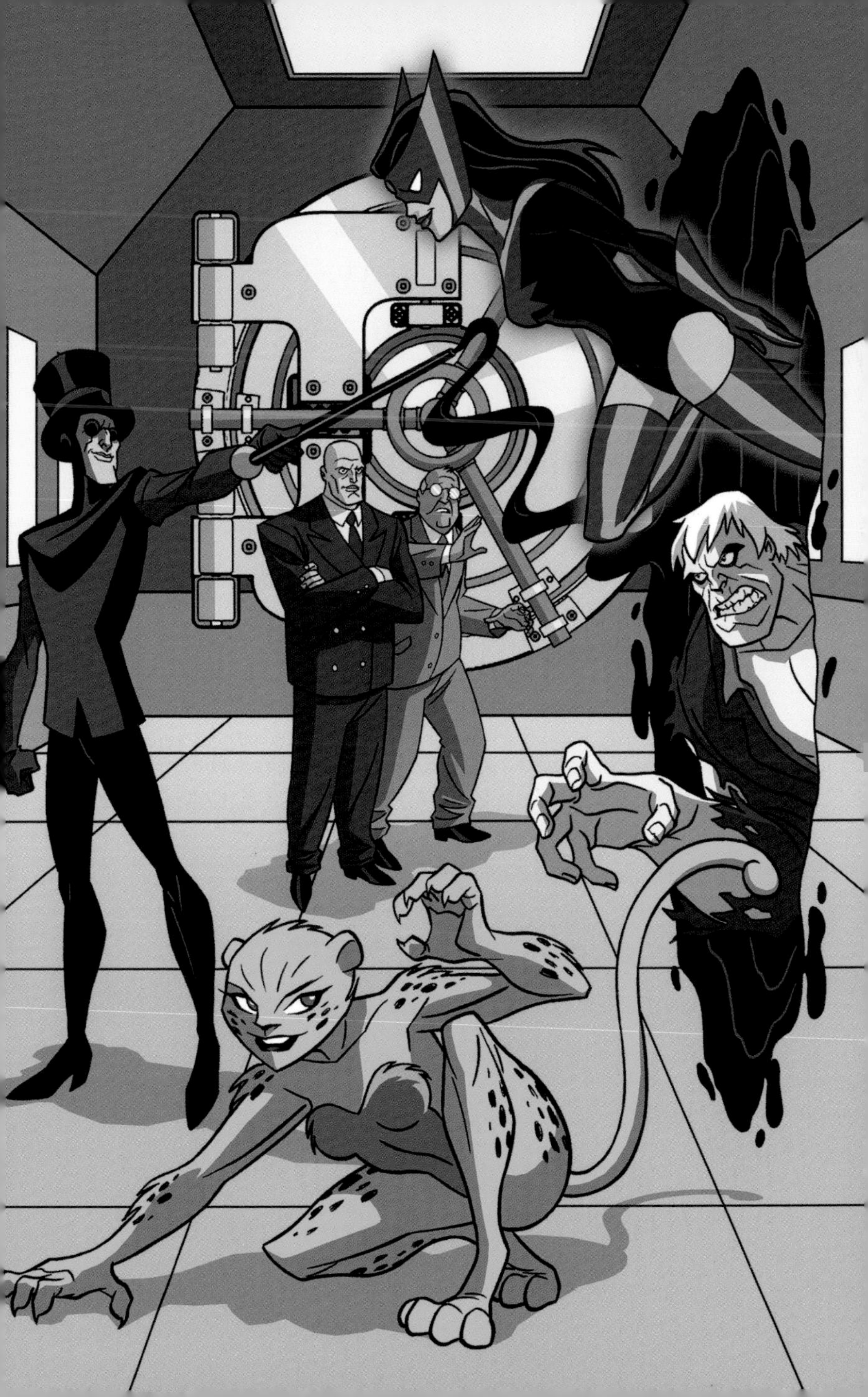

Not to be left behind, the last villain to emerge from the doorway was heard before being seen.

_HA! HA! HA! HA! HA!_

The Clown Prince of Crime's laughter echoed down the hallway. As the Joker stepped from the portal, the infamous Injustice Gang was finally complete.

Drawing their guns, the bank security guards immediately opened fire on the criminals. **_PING! PING! PING!_** The bullets simply bounced off a violet force field created by Star Sapphire.

Using the stone on her mask, Star Sapphire fired an energy beam across the room and into a wall. The shock waves from the blast knocked the guards unconscious. She then destroyed the security cameras with a wide pulse beam.

The Joker danced with glee. "You sure know how to show a guy a good time," he cackled. "Tee hee hee!"

"Quiet, clown!" barked Lex.

The manager was the only bank employee still standing. He quivered in fear as Lex approached him. Star Sapphire hovered alongside the billionaire.

"My crystal stone is powered by love — in this particular case, my love of money," said Star Sapphire with a wicked smile.

"Please . . . don't hurt me," pleaded the bank manager.

"Then open the vault!" demanded Lex. "My patience is wearing thin."

"I can't!" replied the manager. "It runs on a timer. Once in lockdown, it can't be opened until the next business day."

"Allow me," said the Ultra-Humanite, stepping up to the vault and studying it carefully. He pressed his gorilla hand against the cold metal. "He's right. I've studied its inner workings. The vault can't be opened once the lockdown process has begun."

"Let me at it," said Cheetah.

Licking the back of her hand, Cheetah brushed everyone aside to approach the vault door. *MRROWLLL!* She growled as she raked her razor sharp claws across the metal surface. Sparks flew, but her claws didn't make a scratch.

"It can't be opened that way either," said the Ultra-Humanite. "The door is made of 90 tons of compressed steel. Cheetah can't help you, Lex."

"But he can," said Lex, pointing at the hulking zombie. "Grundy, this one is yours."

Solomon Grundy rubbed his chin with a confused look. Trying to decide what to do, he placed his thick hands on the vault's wheel. But instead of spinning it, he pulled. The metal door peeled right off its hinges, opening like an oversized sardine can.

"Grundy open door," mumbled Solomon Grundy with pride.

The bank manager's shoulders slumped with despair. The Joker slid up next to him and playfully pinched his cheek.

"Thank you for playing the wheel of misfortune!" the Joker said, offering his hand. "Put 'er there, kiddo."

ZZZZRRRRKKK!

The instant the Joker shook the manager's hand, a trick buzzer shocked him. The bank manager slumped unconscious to the ground.

Inside the massive vault, stacks of gold bars stood as high as the ceiling. The intense glow from the valuable metal made the Injustice Gang squint.

"We're gonna be rich," said Star Sapphire.

"Grab all of it!" said Lex, leading the gang into the vault. "Don't leave any behind."

"How we take gold without sacks?" asked Grundy, rubbing his chin.

"I was able to transport you all in," said The Shade, waving his cane to open a smaller portal in midair. He then picked up a bar of gold and dropped it into the black hole. It instantly disappeared. "I'll have no problem transporting all of this out."

"That's quite the disappearing act!" said the Joker, shuffling a deck of cards. "Do you know card tricks too?"

"Enough!" yelled Lex. "Let's clean out the vault before anyone else shows up."

"Too late, Lex," said a stern voice behind them.

The Injustice Gang spun around. Superman stood in the vault's doorway, blocking their exit. Behind his billowing cape, the rest of the Justice League approached. Wonder Woman held her golden lasso at the ready as The Flash and the Green Lantern flanked her on either side. Behind them strode Aquaman with his sharp trident and Cyborg with his cybernetic arm constructed into a pulse cannon.

"Where's the bat freak?" asked the Joker with a giggle.

"Behind you," a voice growled.

SMACK!

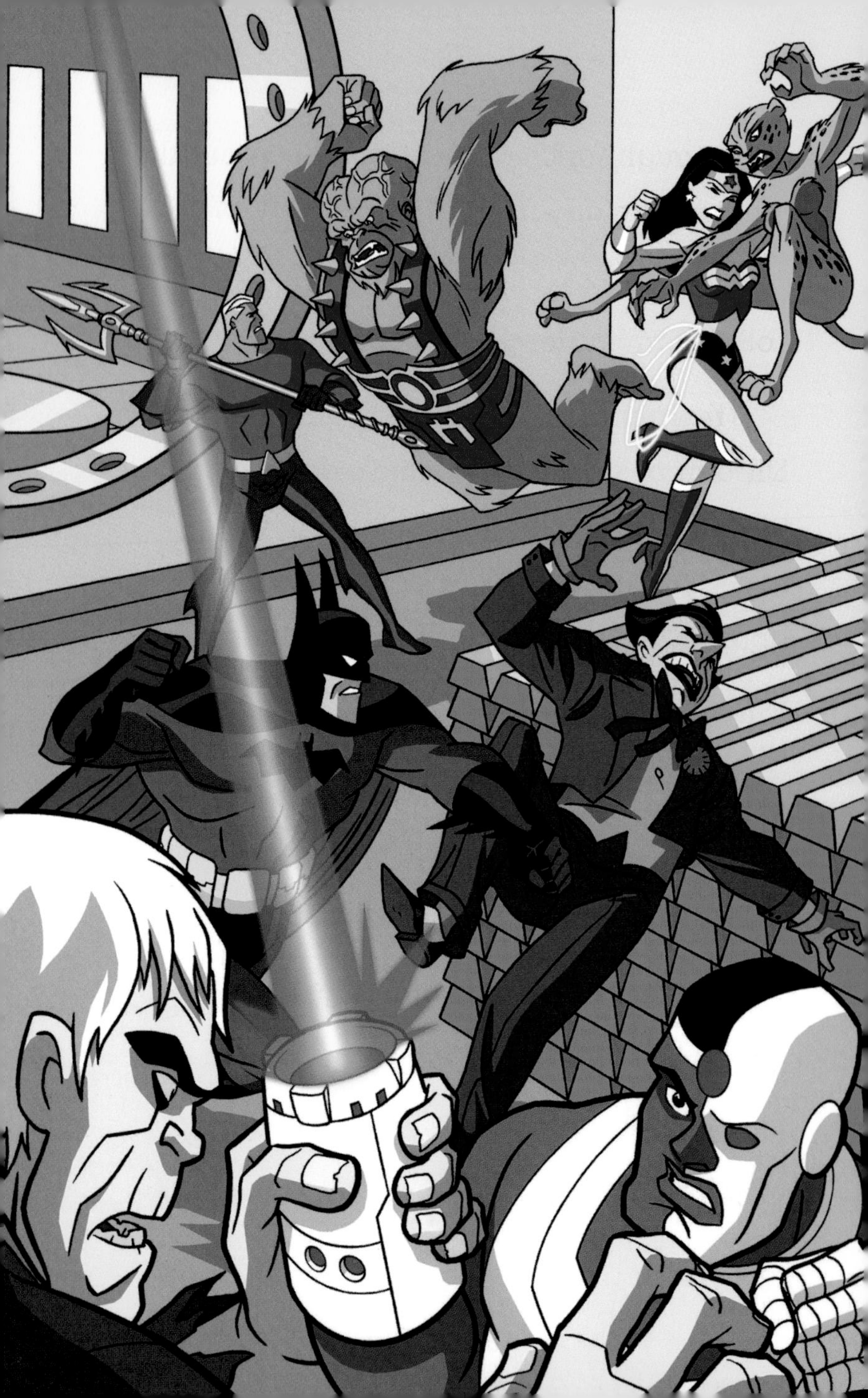

Batman punched the Joker, sending him crashing into a stack of gold bars. *CLANG!*

Racing toward one another, the two teams collided in battle.

"You belong in the ocean," shouted the Ultra-Humanite, leaping at Aquaman.

"And you belong in jail," countered the King of Atlantis. He used his trident, and the gorilla's forward motion, to knock the Ultra-Humanite out of his way.

Nearby, Cheetah tackled Wonder Woman, slashing at her with razor-sharp claws. The Amazon warrior deflected the blows with her bracelets, then kicked the feline villain away. Cheetah somersaulted backward, landed on all fours, and pounced forward again.

"All that glitters is gold," said Cheetah. "They have it. And we want it."

"If that's what you want, then here!" yelled Wonder Woman, tossing her golden lasso around Cheetah to entangle her.

On the opposite side of the vault, Solomon Grundy kicked Cyborg into the wall. As Cyborg crawled back to his feet, a flurry of gold bars flew at him. When one bar hit his metal skull plate, his cybernetic eye crackled with static.

"Hey, quit that!" said Cyborg.

"Robot man no stop Grundy," groaned Solomon.

Cyborg aimed his pulse cannon and fired. The shot hit Grundy in the stomach, taking him down to one knee. As Grundy rose to his feet, a red blur and burst of wind swirled around him. When the villain took a step forward, he tripped and fell face-first into the ground. His shoelaces had been tied together.

"Booyah!" exclaimed Cyborg, giving The Flash a high-five for his help.

Meanwhile, green and violet light shot across the vault as Green Lantern and Star Sapphire circled in midair. Beneath them, Superman walked toward Lex Luthor, backing the criminal mastermind up against a stack of gold bars.

"It's over, Lex," said Superman. "Turn yourself in. There's no way out."

"You underestimate us," replied Luthor.

Pressing a button on his wristwatch, green and purple armor deployed and encased Luthor's body. His superpowered metal suit was now a match for the Man of Steel.

Luthor locked arms with Superman. His powerful grip forced the Man of Steel down to his knees.

"Why, Lex?" asked Superman, straining to stand back up. "You're already rich. Why steal the gold?"

"Why not?" replied Lex. "No one has ever successfully robbed this Federal Reserve. My team is here for the gold. I'm here for the bragging rights."

Lex tossed Superman aside. Then he focused his hands on Green Lantern, shooting an energy blast that knocked the hero into a pile of gold. An avalanche of bars tumbled down, trapping Green Lantern underneath.

Using the opening created by Lex, Star Sapphire made a giant vise with her crystal stone. Herding the Justice League together, she attempted to crush them. As they struggled against the vise, The Shade raised his cane and pointed it in their direction.

"Darkness is a prison of my creation," said The Shade. "With the absence of light, you'll stay there . . . forever."

Before he could command the darkness, a Batarang zipped across the vault. It struck the cane, knocking it out of The Shade's hands. When the cane hit the ground, it shattered like glass across the vault floor.

Immediately the room plunged into total darkness.

"We're out of here — now!" shouted Lex. "Star Sapphire, could you do the honors?"

A violet light suddenly pierced the darkness, growing from a tiny ball above Star Sapphire's head to a large orb that encased the Injustice Gang. Lifting the villains into the air, it carried them from the vault and into the dead of night. Their escape left the Justice League behind in total darkness.

CHAPTER 2

ENTER THE SHADOWLANDS

The vault remained pitch black as the Justice League stumbled around in the dark.

"Is everyone okay?" asked Wonder Woman.

"I am," answered the Man of Steel.

"I as well," said Aquaman.

"Same here," replied Cyborg. "Although my cybernetic eye is disabled."

"I'm okay. How about you, Batman?" asked The Flash.

"I'm fine," responded Batman. "But my flashlight isn't working."

"Where's Green Lantern?" asked Superman, realizing he hadn't heard anything from his friend.

"Over here," called Batman. "He's trapped under a pile of gold bars. Follow my voice. Help me get him out."

The Flash felt his way over to the pile. With a burst of speed, his hands zipped back and forth, lifting the gold bars and restacking them off to the side. A weak groan rose from the floor.

UUUGGHHH!

"I . . . must've hit my head . . . really hard," murmured Green Lantern. "All I can see . . . is black." Wonder Woman reached down to help pull him back to his feet.

"It's not just you, buddy," said The Flash. "Those Injustice losers turned out the lights."

Pointing his fist into the air, Green Lantern created a large hovering lantern with his ring. The heroes used its green light to guide them out of the vault and down a long hallway toward the front of the bank.

When the Justice League stepped outside the Federal Reserve building, they stopped in their tracks. All of Metropolis was dark too.

"How long were we in there?" asked The Flash. "Is it nighttime already?"

"It can't be," replied Superman. "We weren't in the vault that long. Besides, there's no moon or stars in the sky."

"Or any lights coming from anywhere," noted Aquaman. "No streetlights or buildings are lit up."

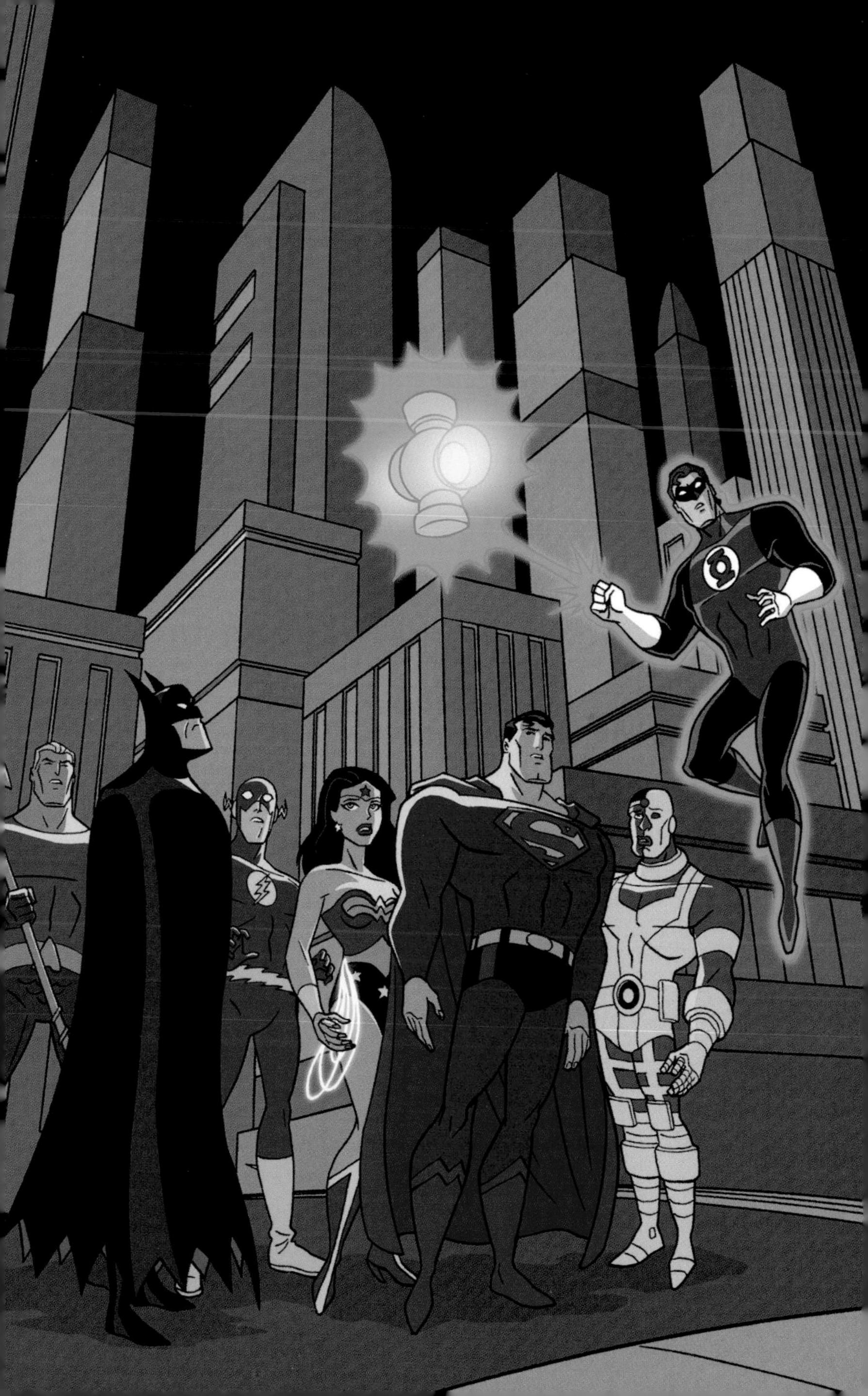

"I think I know why," said Batman. "The Shade harnesses his powers through his cane. During the battle, my Batarang destroyed it. I think that disrupted its powers, driving away all the light and plunging us into darkness."

"Not all the light," corrected Green Lantern, making a fist as his ring glowed.

"Is this darkness permanent?" asked Wonder Woman. "If the cane was destroyed, how can we return things to normal?"

KA·BOOOOM!

An explosion erupted a few blocks away. Its flash of light pierced the darkness for a moment.

"That blast came from the direction of the First National Bank," said Superman. "First we deal with that. Then we'll figure out how to bring back the light."

Using his ring, Green Lantern created a bubble around the Justice League and carried them toward the explosion. When they arrived, they found the front of the bank blown open. Then the Injustice Gang stepped out with bags stuffed with cash. They were taking advantage of the city's darkness.

"This is a fire sale. Everything must go!" the Joker laughed as loose bills spilled from his bag.

"No more thieving!" commanded the Man of Steel. "Lex, this stops now!"

"The time of bright heroes has been extinguished, Superman," proclaimed Lex. "Now only darkness remains."

"That's what you think," said Green Lantern. He created a giant barred prison of light, then dropped it over the Injustice Gang. It kept all from escaping — except one.

The Shade ran into an alley, thinking he had escaped. But Batman silently stalked him from behind. Grabbing his collar, the Dark Knight thrust him against the wall.

"Shade! You must fix this!" said Batman. "Eternal darkness will doom our planet."

"It's out of my control. You broke my cane and cast the world into deadly nightshade," said The Shade. "Now the Shadowlands have taken over."

"Shadowlands?" asked Batman.

"The darkest place from which I draw my powers. Now loose, my power will take over the world," said The Shade. "My shadows are free to become anything . . . and anyone!"

Batman looked back at his teammates. Stunned by what he saw, the Dark Knight released his grip on The Shade.

The light from Green Lantern's ring cast the Justice League's shadows against the bank wall. But something wasn't right. Their dark silhouettes had actually detached from the wall. Evil duplicates, courtesy of the Shadowlands, began to walk on their own. The Shade's warning had become a evil reality.

Immediately the duplicates swarmed Green Lantern, forcing him to break his concentration. His green jail of light dissolved, setting the Injustice Gang free. They fled into the streets of Metropolis, carrying away their stolen cash.

The shadow duplicates then turned their attention on their hosts. Wonder Woman and Aquaman tried to wrestle their duplicates, but the heroes simply passed right through them.

The Flash attempted to outrun his, but it tripped him up no matter which direction he ran. When Cyborg blasted his shadow with his photon cannon, it sunk into the ground. Then it reappeared beneath him and shorted out his circuitry.

"Everyone take cover!" yelled the Man of Steel, as he flew into the air. Using his laser vision, Superman fired on each shadow duplicate. Every successful hit drove away one shadow, but caused two more to reform in its place. Over and over he shot, but more and more shadows sprung to life.

Without the Sun to recharge his powers, Superman's energy began to fade. Exhausted from the use of his laser vision, he passed out. His tired and heavy body plummeted to the hard concrete.

CRA-KOOM!

"Superman!" yelled Wonder Woman, struggling free from her shadowy duplicate.

"He's unconscious but otherwise okay," confirmed Batman, bending down to check on his friend. "But we need an exit strategy . . . NOW!"

"The harbor is near here," said Aquaman, sniffing the air. "I can smell the salt water. Follow me!"

Batman hoisted Superman onto his shoulder and the Justice League followed Aquaman toward the sea. The army of shadow duplicates trailed them in pursuit.

When they arrived at the docks, the team ran out of room. They stood at the edge of a short pier overlooking the ocean. The shadow duplicates paused for a moment, sensing something was out of place.

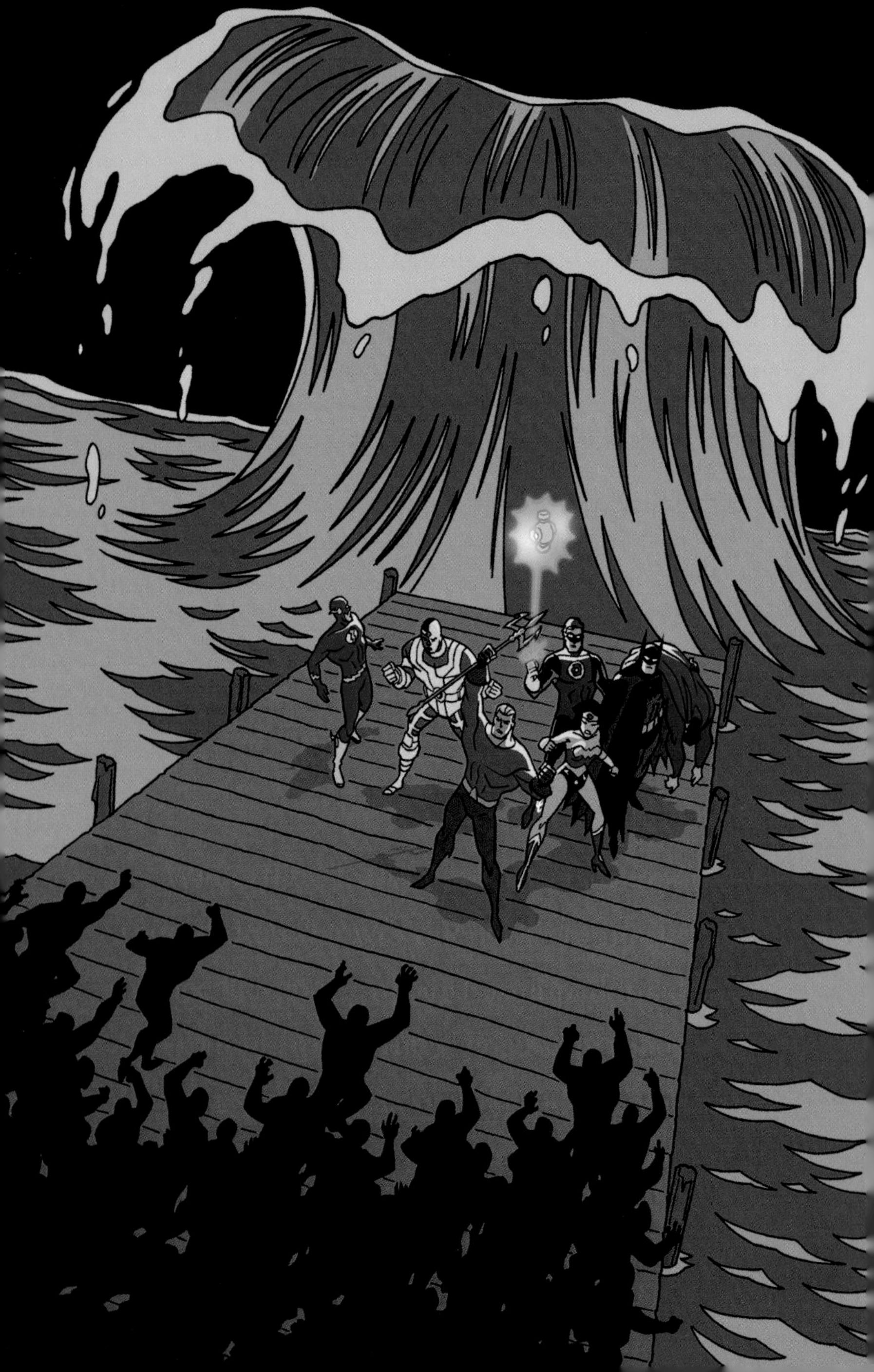

"I think we missed the boat," said The Flash.

"No! We make our stand right here," commanded Aquaman. "Now you'll see why I'm king of this sea!"

As the shadow duplicates charged, Aquaman raised his trident into the air. The ocean went still, as if listening. Then the foamy tide suddenly rose one hundred feet into the air behind them and crashed down onto the docks. The controlled wave washed away the shadow duplicates but left the Justice League dry and unharmed.

The heroes were safe for now. But with Superman unconscious, where could they find safety in a world without light?

CHAPTER 3

COLD RETREAT

A chill wind blew across the Arctic tundra as the seven heroes trudged through the snow. Moments before, they had arrived in a jet of Green Lantern's creation. Now his power ring had created a giant searchlight. Its long green beam lit the way to their final destination — a mountain of ice.

"It's no Bat-Signal, but it'll light our way," said Green Lantern.

"Are we close?" asked Batman, carrying a weary Superman on his back.

"Up . . . ahead," the Man of Steel replied, his voice soft and weak.

"It wuh-wuh-would've been . . . a better idea . . . to go to the Watchtower instead," said The Flash through chattering teeth. "Why . . . cuh-cuh-come all the way . . . out here?"

"The alien technology in Superman's home may make it the only place that still has power," said Wonder Woman. "And it may have what Superman needs to recover."

Soon they arrived at the base of an ice mountain that rose hundreds of feet above them. Its outer wall looked completely smooth, except for a large metal slab with a peculiar shape carved in its center.

"My cyber eye still doesn't work, but my good eye does. Is that what I think it is?" asked Cyborg, pointing up at the wall.

In the light cast by Green Lantern's ring, the shape appeared to be a giant key hole.

"Duh-duh-don't look at me," stuttered The Flash. "I left my keys . . . in my other pants."

Batman put Superman down to conduct a search. After prodding the ground around him, he began wiping away loose snow. Gradually, a metal object began to emerge.

"A little wind over here would help," said Batman.

The Flash extended both arms straight out and began twirling them. His swirling vortex blew the powdery snow away and revealed a giant metal key.

"That's some doormat," said The Flash, kicking away one last clump of snow.

"It looks heavy," said Aquaman. He wedged his trident underneath the key to pry it up, but it wouldn't budge. "As I thought. It's something only Superman can lift."

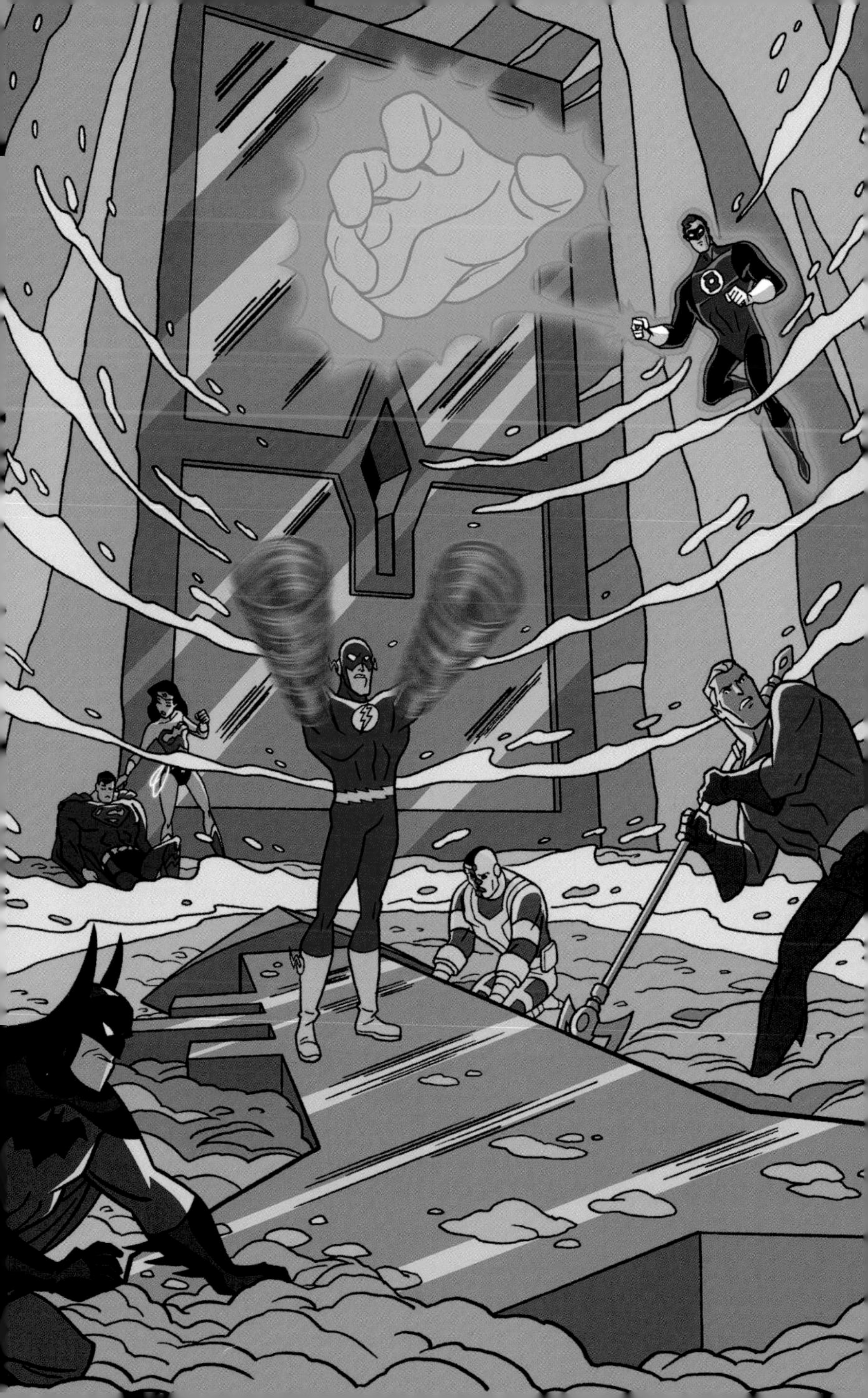

"Let me try," said Cyborg, whose enhanced body was stronger than any normal man's. Grabbing the key with both hands, he strained with all his might. The key rose an inch off the ground then fell back into the snow.

CHOOOOM!

"Let me lend you a hand," said Green Lantern. Using his power ring to create a giant glowing hand, he picked up the huge key, slid it into the lock, and turned it.

CLICK!

The latch unlocked, sending a shudder down the frozen doorway. A shower of snowflakes sprinkled to the ground as the door slowly creaked open.

"Open sesame!" said Green Lantern. "Now let's get out of this blasted cold."

Carrying Superman on his back, Batman led the rest of the Justice League through the giant doorway. Once inside, the door closed behind them.

BA-BOOOOM!

A loud echo shook the long tunnel they stood in.

With only one direction to go, the Justice League followed the tunnel deeper into the mountain. Soon, a light at the end of the passageway led them into a huge room. The heroes shielded their eyes from the glare dancing off every icy surface.

Superman's Fortress of Solitude was truly a sight to behold. In the entryway, two giant stone statues held up a replica of the planet Krypton. Along one wall, an ice-carved stairway led up to a zoo holding orphaned creatures from across the galaxy.

In the center of the room a bed of crystal shards stood on a platform near a giant supercomputer. High above them, the rocket that had carried Superman to Earth as a baby hung between the stalactites.

"And here I thought only Batman had a crazy cave collection," said The Flash.

Without warning, a robot with red glowing eyes rolled toward them. Cyborg raised his photon cannon in defense, but Batman waved him down. The robot's chest was imprinted with an S-shield. It wasn't a threat.

"WELCOME, JUSTICE LEAGUE," the robot said in a flat, mechanical voice. "HOW MAY I ASSIST?"

"Our friend is hurt," Batman said, placing Superman into the robot's metal arms. "Can you help him?"

The robot's eyes turned blue as it scanned his body. "HIS CELLS LACK THEIR NEEDED CHARGE," it concluded. "HE NEEDS THE RAYS OF THE SUN."

The Justice League followed the robot into a nearby medical chamber. It placed Superman onto a flat table beneath a small floating yellow orb. No larger than a baseball, the orb pulsated, bathing Superman with light energy.

"THIS POCKET SUN WILL RESTORE HIS HEALTH," the robot explained. Then it turned to Cyborg. "MAY I REPAIR YOU?"

"Sure," said Cyborg. "Just be careful around the eye. It's the most damaged."

The robot's hand slid open, changing into an array of medical tools. Using a power drill, a mini-laser, and wired circuitry, it performed surgery on Cyborg's damaged eye.

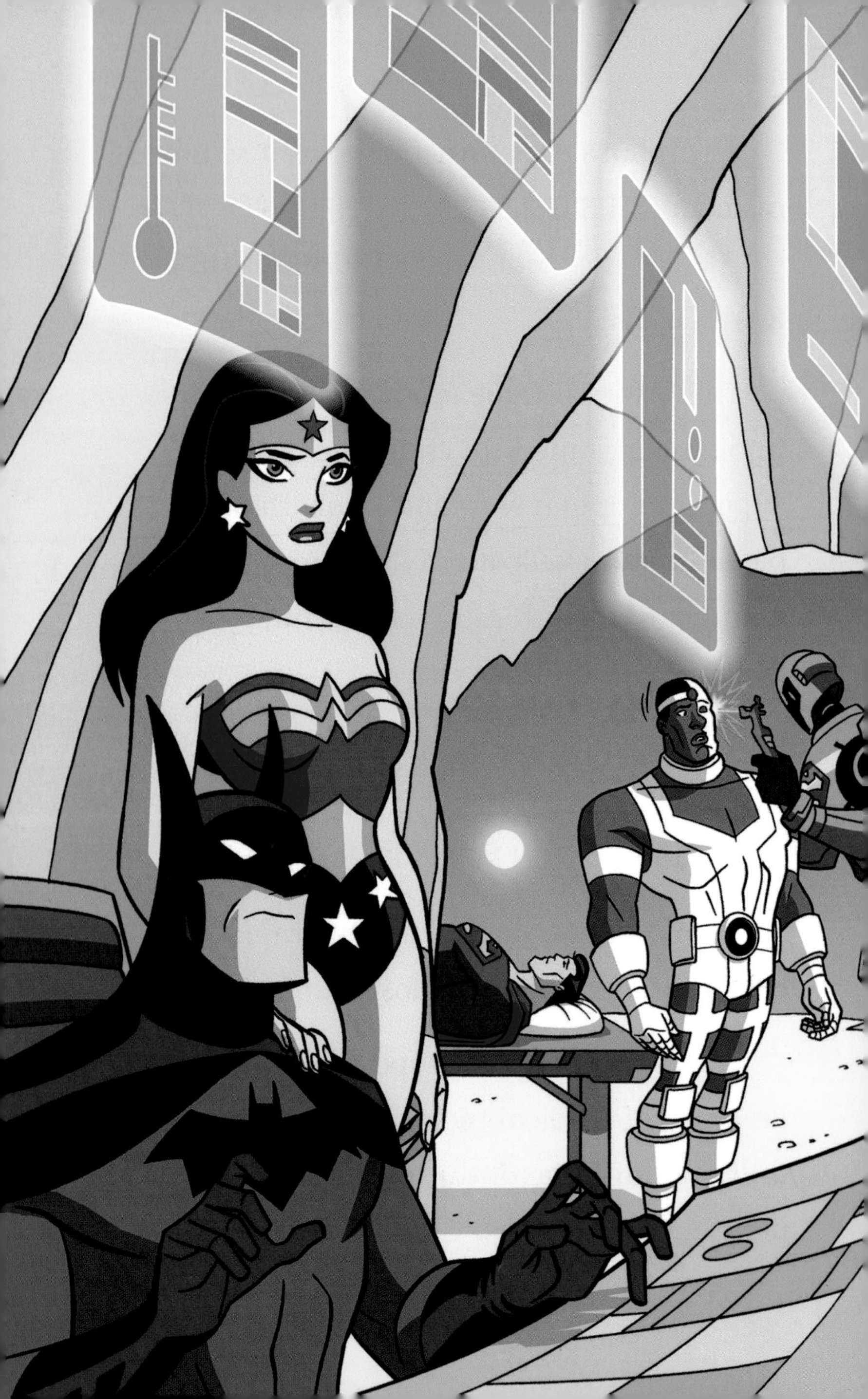

While Superman and Cyborg received medical attention, Batman walked back into the main room. He used the supercomputer to collect data from their Watchtower satellite in space. One chart that popped up on the screen included a blinking thermometer.

"What is it?" asked Wonder Woman, placing her hand on Batman's shoulder.

"Without the Sun, Earth's temperature is dropping . . ." Batman trailed off as images filled the screen. Snow covered the Sahara Desert. Ice blanketed the Sphinx in Egypt. A blizzard held Metropolis in an icy grip.

"If the spell created by The Shade's cane continues at this rate, Earth could be facing a new Ice Age," said the Dark Knight.

"As King of Atlantis, I am prepared to offer whatever refuge I can for Earth's people," said Aquaman, stepping forward.

"I as well," said Wonder Woman. "My home island of Themyscira would welcome as many as it could."

"Both are generous offers," said a familiar voice from the medical chamber behind them.

"Superman!" exclaimed Wonder Woman.

With his health restored, the Man of Steel entered the main room. "But we're looking for a solution. Not just a temporary fix."

Batman stroked his chin in silence, staring at the icy floor. After a moment his head bobbed up.

"I have an idea," the Caped Crusader finally said. "But you're not going to like it."

"What does it involve?" asked Superman.

"We're going to prison," said Batman. "There's someone we need to break out."

CHAPTER 4
EARLY PAROLE

Carried in Green Lantern's ball of light, the Justice League touched down on the dark, wet ground just outside Belle Reve Penitentiary. The building was a featureless block of grim concrete located in the middle of Louisiana. Tall guard towers placed at each corner connected the electrified fences that surrounded the complex. Anyone lucky enough to escape through them would be forced to slog through gator-infested swamplands for miles around.

"What a lovely setting you've brought us to," said Wonder Woman, wrinkling her nose.

The emerald light cast by Green Lantern's ring had a way of making everything look gloomier.

"You know, Belle Reve is French for 'beautiful dream,'" replied Batman.

"More like ugly nightmare," muttered The Flash.

"It doesn't matter what it looks like on the outside," Batman said. "The person we need is inside."

Not wasting a moment, Aquaman swung his trident at the metal fence.

"Wait," Superman yelled. "That fence is electri —"

But his warning came too late. The King of Atlantis slashed the fence apart. But aside from opening a hole large enough to walk through, nothing else happened.

"Of course!" said The Flash, smacking his forehead. "The power's out!"

"Without electricity, the facility's other security systems have likely failed as well," said Aquaman, leading the way through the hole in the fence. "What do you think is happening inside the prison?"

BANG!

As if answering his question, the front doors of the prison suddenly burst open. A small group of inmates in orange jumpsuits rushed outside. But the joy on their faces from their newfound freedom quickly faded. The instant they spotted the Justice League, they turned on their heels and ran back inside the prison.

"Who needs electricity to keep the inmates in line?" said The Flash.

The Justice League followed the inmates through the front doors and found the facility engulfed in a full-fledged riot. All of the prison cell doors had swung open, and the inmates were running free. Screaming and gunfire could be heard throughout the hallways deep within the facility.

"This riot is going to make finding the criminal I need tougher," said Batman. "We must hurry!"

As they rounded a corner, a large group of inmates blocked a wide hallway lined with prison cells.

"Go to your cells now!" yelled Superman. His command fell on deaf ears.

The inmates charged forward like a surging wave. Aquaman used his trident to pin the first prisoner against the wall.

Wonder Woman lassoed an inmate, then used his momentum to swing him into three more inmates. She toppled them like bowling pins.

Superman even unleashed a blast of his super-breath, but it wasn't enough to hold back the tide of prisoners. No matter how many inmates the Justice League knocked down, even more kept coming.

"You got your warning," said Green Lantern. "Now accept your punishment." He used his ring to make a giant green bulldozer. Then he drove it toward the inmates, pushing them all backward. "It's your turn, Flash!"

The Flash sped into the fray and grabbed each inmate by his collar. He crisscrossed the hallway in a blur of red, depositing the escapees into every open prison cell.

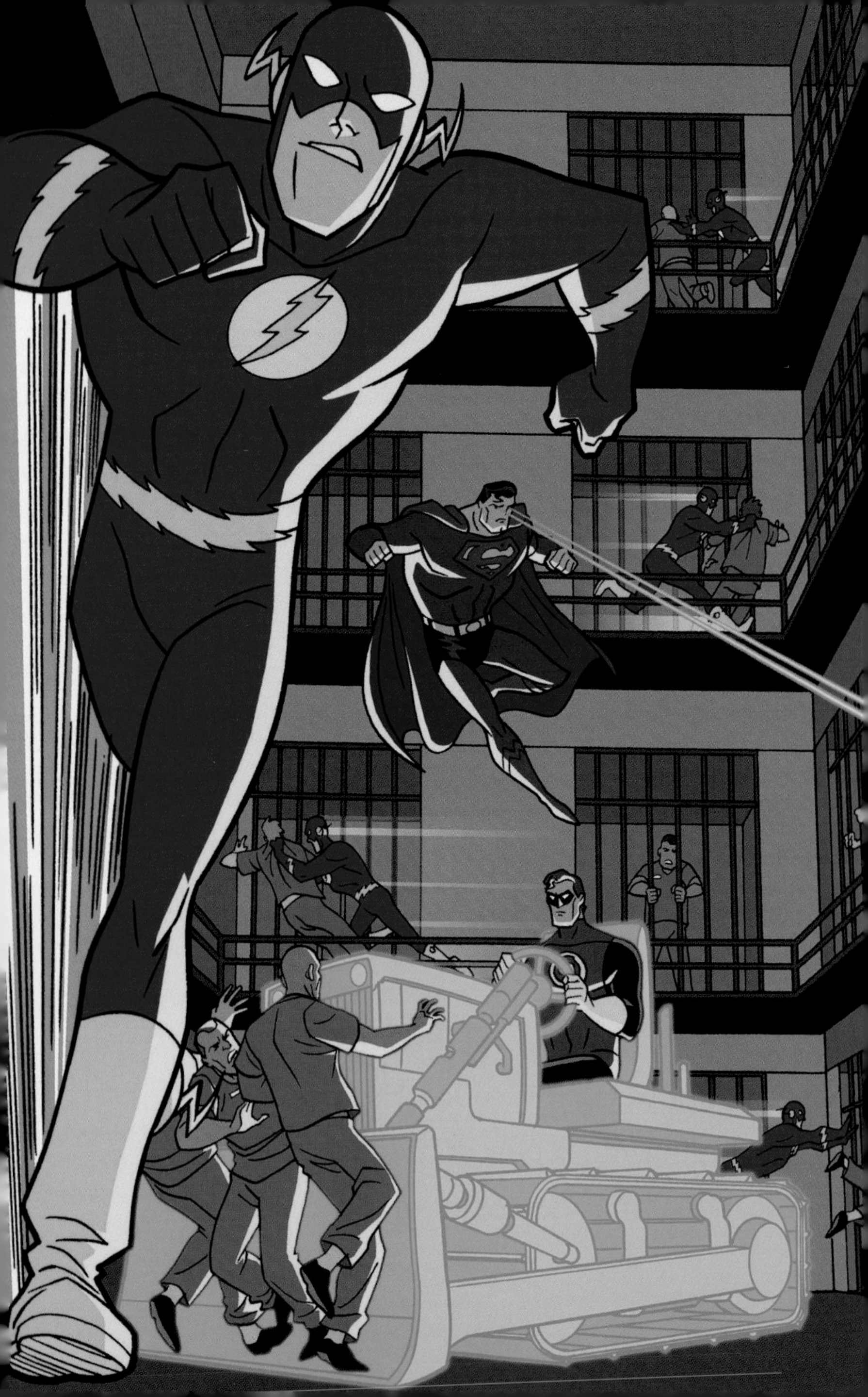

Within seconds, The Flash had cleared the hallway and filled the cells. Then Superman used his heat vision to melt each cell door's lock in place.

"That should hold them," said the Man of Steel.

"Where to next?" asked Aquaman, turning to Batman.

"The cafeteria," answered the Dark Knight. "We'll have to go through there to get to the other side of the building."

The sounds of a fierce battle got louder as they approached the cafeteria. They stopped just outside its doors, preparing for what was on the other side.

"My cybernetic eye is picking up multiple heat signatures inside," groaned Cyborg. "Not a lot of friendlies."

They swung open the doors and stepped into a war zone. Lunch tables had been made into barricades around the room. Scared security guards crouched behind a wall of tables along one side. Inmates hid and attacked from the other.

The Justice League took cover with the security guards. Amanda Waller, who ran Belle Reve, was among them.

"The power grid is down across the state," said Waller, scowling at Superman. "I'm guessing your group is responsible for that."

"Keep your head down, Miss Waller," said Superman, sensing her distrust. "We're here to help."

"Right," replied Waller, shaking her head. "More like whenever there's a problem in this world, one of you is always to blame!"

CRACK!

A bullet shattered the lip of the table Waller crouched behind.

"I'd take his advice if I were you," said Batman.

The gunshot had been fired by Floyd Lawton, better known as the accurate assassin Deadshot. He hid behind a barricade of tables with Harley Quinn, the Joker's lovesick sidekick. Next to her crouched Killer Croc, a criminal with rough, scaly crocodile skin, and Captain Boomerang, a master at throwing the classic Aussie hunting weapon.

"Hey lucky! I thought ya never missed a shot," teased Harley.

"I don't," replied Floyd with a smirk. "That was just a warning shot. Purely intentional. Where'd you get that, slugger?"

"Storage locker," answered Harley Quinn, showing off the baseball bat in her hands. "My cell block softball team won the championship."

"You're in a league of your own, aren't you, Harley?" said Floyd.

"Don'tcha know it!" replied Harley with a wide smile.

"Crikey! Will you two shut up and let the rest of us have some fun." Captain Boomerang chuckled. He jumped up and tossed a bent stick fashioned from a table leg toward a guard. The makeshift boomerang circled behind the guard and struck him in the back of the head, knocking him out.

"This is a cafeteria, isn't it?" growled Croc. "Time to eat!" He leaped from behind a table and charged a group of guards.

"Not tonight, Croc," shouted Batman, who swung across the room on a grapnel line. He used his forward motion to kick the villain across the jaw.

Wiping his mouth, Croc backhanded Batman into an overturned table. Then he jumped on top of him, pinning the Dark Knight to the ground.

CHOMP! CHOMP! His jaws snapped inches from Batman's cowl.

"Dinner's served and bats are on the menu!" Croc laughed. He opened his mouth wide, preparing to bite.

"The kitchen is closed," said Aquaman, using a choke hold to pull Croc off Batman.

"Get offa me, fish boy!" growled Croc.

Aquaman laughed. "I've wrestled bigger piranhas than you."

Batman removed a small bottle from his Utility Belt and sprayed it in Croc's face. The knock-out gas instantly put him to sleep.

SWISH! SWISH!

A makeshift boomerang whistled over Batman's head, narrowly missing him. Another zipped toward Aquaman, cutting him across the cheek. Both heroes dove in opposite directions to get out of range.

"Look at 'em hop away. This is just like huntin' kangaroos down under," bragged Captain Boomerang. He threw another volley of three spinning boomerangs. But as each one neared its target, a red blur snatched it out of the air.

"Here ya go," said The Flash, carrying all three back to Captain Boomerang. "I think you lost these." Then he clonked the villain in the back of the head, knocking him out.

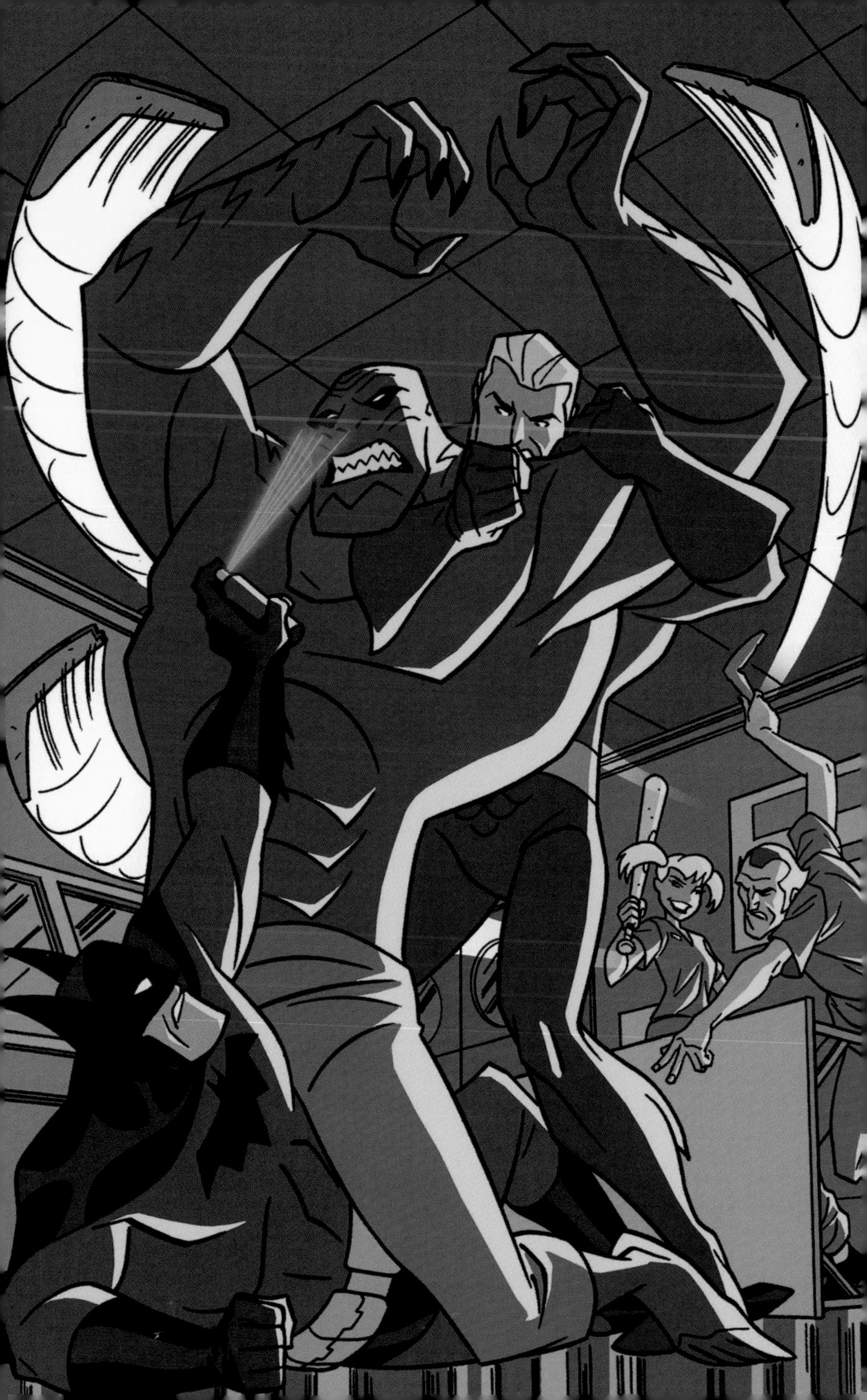

As Deadshot continued to fire in Waller's direction, Green Lantern made a knight's shield to protect her and the guards. Then Cyborg stepped forward to provide cover by shooting his photon cannon in Deadshot and Harley's direction. His attack gave Wonder Woman a chance to rush into battle.

BANG! BANG! BANG!

Deadshot fired multiple shots, emptying his gun at Wonder Woman. But the Amazing Amazon deflected every bullet with her silver bracelets. With nothing left to shoot, Deadshot turned to run. **SWOOSH!** Wonder Woman's magic lasso tripped him up.

"Now that wasn't very nice," said Harley Quinn, standing behind the Amazon warrior, winding up with her baseball bat. "It's the bottom of the ninth and here comes the grand slam!"

Harley swung her baseball bat at Wonder Woman, who instinctively raised her wrists to protect herself. When the bat collided with the hero's bracelets, it splintered into pieces.

"One strike," Wonder Woman said, throwing a punch that knocked Harley to the ground. "You're out!"

Moments later, all of the cafeteria inmates were recaptured. Wonder Woman tied them up in her rope.

Amanda Waller scanned the room. "I guess thanks are in order," she mumbled.

"Sorry, we couldn't hear you," said The Flash, leaning closer to the annoyed prison director. "Care to repeat that?"

"Take these prisoners back to their cells," Waller ordered her security guards. Then she turned back to the Justice League.

"Visiting hours are over. I want the rest of you off this property right now," Waller barked. "And that goes double for Batman, wherever he is. Round him up, or I will!"

"Is this one of his famous disappearing acts?" Wonder Woman asked the Man of Steel in a hushed tone.

"He must have gone for the prisoner he's after!" Superman whispered back.

* * *

On the other side of the prison, Batman moved down the hall like a ghost. Even in darkness, the Caped Crusader knew his way around this facility. He had brought many of its inmates here personally. Still, he reached into his Utility Belt and removed a flare. Lighting it, he walked to the end of the hall and stopped in front of a closed door.

The Dark Knight took a long breath. Then he placed his hand against the door and pushed it open.

"It's about time," said an irritated voice from inside. "If your appointment was with me, then you're late."

The inmate rose to his feet. Clearly not a physical threat, the thin older man stepped into the light.

"And no one makes the Clock King wait!"

THE LAST TIME

TICK! TOCK! TICK! TOCK!

Ticking clocks of every kind sounded together all around the room. A large grandfather clock leaned against the wall. A windup cuckoo clock fluttered its doors, revealing a tiny wooden bird. A cat clock kept perfect time with its shifty eyes and swinging tail.

The Justice League stood in the private apartment of Temple Fugate, the villain better known as the Clock King. And his workspace was being used for a very important job.

The Clock King had changed from his orange prison jumpsuit and into his typical clothing. A derby hat covered his balding head. A pair of clock-faced round glasses covered his eyes. A dark tie and a buttoned suit the color of the wood finish on an antique clock covered his thin frame.

Aside from a flashlight created by Green Lantern, candles afforded the only light to the room. The world outside was still cold, dark, and without power.

"Fugate, your technology has stopped time in the past. Even sped it up," said Batman. "I'm hoping you have something here that can reverse time as well."

"Even if I did, why would I help you?" asked the Clock King, raising an eyebrow. "Perhaps I've got more important things to do with my time."

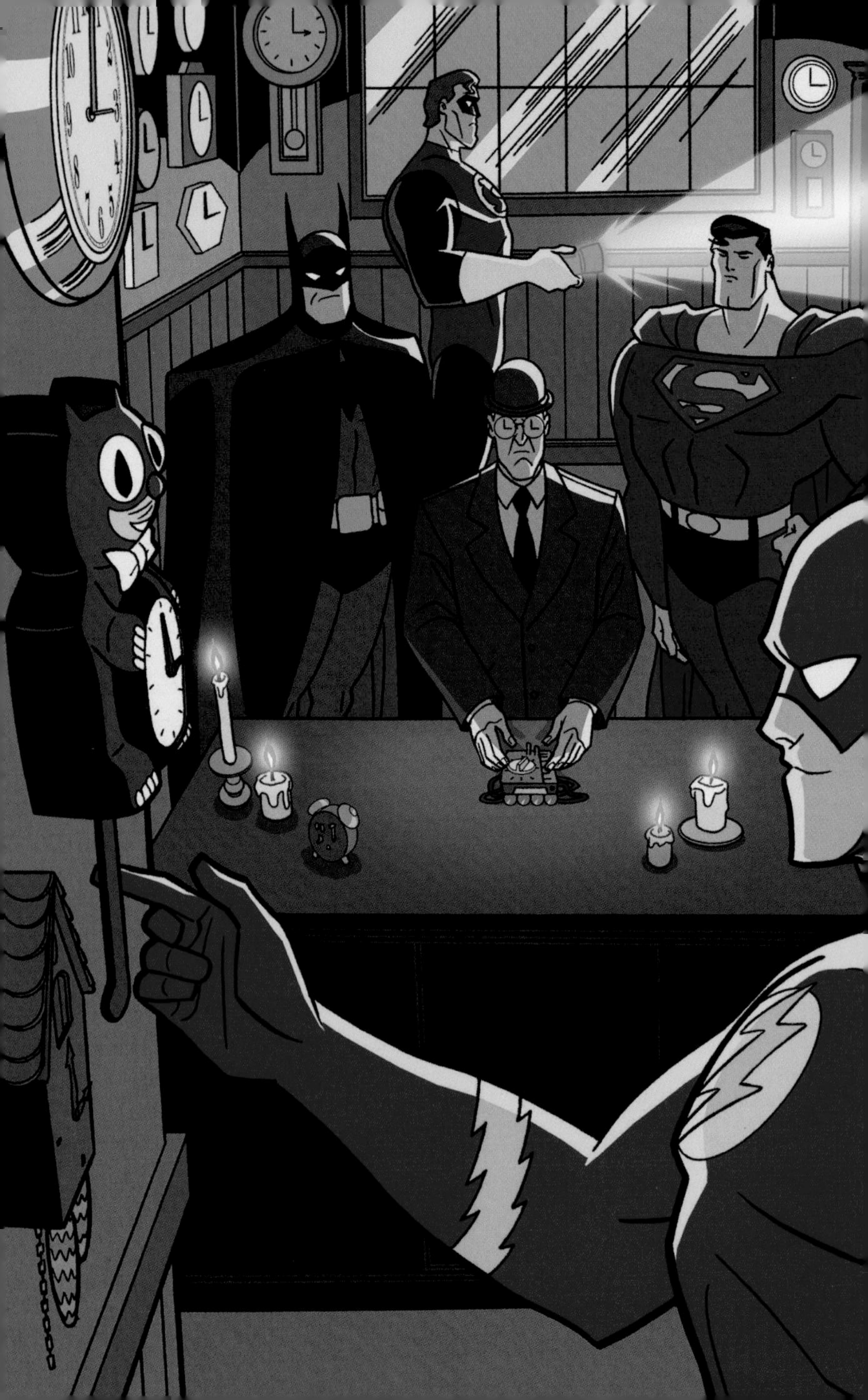

"While you were locked up in Belle Reve, there was . . . an incident. One that has created eternal darkness," explained Batman. "With it comes no more safety. No more order. Without that . . . time is meaningless."

The Clock King reached inside his suit coat and removed a gold pocket watch on a chain. He wound it nervously. "I see your point," he finally replied.

The Clock King opened a desk drawer, removed a small rectangular device, and placed it on the desktop. The device had a dial in the middle that needed to be wound. Several wires were wrapped around the device. They attached an ionized atomic battery to its back.

"This was something I was working on," said the Clock King, "before our last untimely interruption."

"You were trying to blow up Gotham City Hall before I stopped you," said Batman, squinting his eyes.

Ignoring the Dark Knight's response, Fugate continued. "This device removes electrons from molecules in the air. Then it converts them into tacheon particles."

"It's a time machine!" exclaimed the Caped Crusader.

"Wrong! It's a time . . . window," corrected Fugate. "It can't create an opening large enough for a person to enter. Instead, it can open a small window through time for only three seconds. To be of much use, it must be activated at the exact location you want to see in the past."

"That's it? What good will that do?" complained The Flash, throwing his hands in the air.

"We'll make it work. It's our only shot," said Superman. "Thank you, Mr. Fugate."

Batman attached the time device to his Utility Belt.

"Remember . . . time waits for no man," warned the Clock King.

"For you it will," said Batman as he handcuffed the Clock King to his desk.

"Speaking of which, it's time for us to go back to the Federal Reserve Bank," said Superman. He turned to Green Lantern. "Can you give the team one last lift?"

"Sure thing," replied Green Lantern.

Outside the Clock King's apartment, Green Lantern created a jet aircraft with his ring. The Justice League climbed inside and flew back to Metropolis, leaving a glowing green light trail in the dark sky.

When they arrived, the street outside the Federal Reserve was silent and empty. The Justice League cautiously stepped inside the bank to return to the scene of the incident. It was exactly how they left it. The vault door was peeled open. An avalanche of gold bars remained piled on the floor.

Using Green Lantern's ring as a spotlight, Batman found the shards of The Shade's shattered cane. Retracing his steps, he located the spot where he had stood when he threw his Batarang.

"Here!" said the Dark Knight. "This is where it happened."

"Are you certain?" asked Superman.

"Positive," replied Batman. "Get ready. When I turn the Clock King's device on, we'll have only a heartbeat to stop my Batarang from destroying the cane."

The Dark Knight removed the time device from his Utility Belt, turned the dial, and pressed a button. A motor hummed softly inside the device.

"Let's hope this works," said The Flash with his fingers crossed.

Batman stared straight ahead. "We'll know in three seconds."

* * *

Inside the Federal Reserve Bank vault, the Injustice Gang prepared to take all the gold. They just needed a way to do it.

"I was able to transport you all in," said The Shade, waving his cane to open a small portal in midair. He then picked up a bar of gold and dropped it into the black hole. It instantly disappeared. "I'll have no problem transporting all of this out."

"That's quite the disappearing act!" said the Joker, shuffling a deck of cards. "Do you know card tricks too?"

"Enough!" yelled Lex. "Let's clean out the vault before anyone else shows up."

"Too late, Lex," said a stern voice behind them.

The Injustice Gang spun around. Superman and the Justice League stood in the vault's doorway, blocking their exit.

"Where's the bat freak?" asked Joker with a giggle.

"Behind you," a voice growled.

SMACK!

Batman punched the Joker, sending him crashing into a stack of gold bars.

CLANG!

As the rest of the Justice League fought the Injustice Gang, Batman kept to the shadows. He hid behind stacks of gold, moving closer to his target.

The Dark Knight's focus was on The Shade, who was now only one stack of gold away. The villain dropped one gold bar after another inside his black portal while his cohorts battled the Justice League.

Suddenly, Star Sapphire imprisoned the Justice League inside a giant purple vise. The Shade paused for a moment and pointed his cane in their direction.

"Darkness is a prison of my creation. With the absence of light, you'll stay there forever," The Shade threatened.

Unable to wait a moment longer, Batman threw a Batarang at The Shade's cane to interrupt the spell.

At the exact same moment, a small brilliant window of light, not unlike The Shade's portal of darkness, opened above the Dark Knight. The glare blinded The Shade, causing him to pause before using his cane. In that heartbeat, a pair of red lasers shot through the window, striking the Batarang in midair. The Batarang deflected harmlessly to the ground, and the window of light closed.

Seeing his Batarang miss its mark, Batman climbed over the pile of gold bars, leaped off it, and unfurled his winged cape. He tackled The Shade. As The Shade squirmed on the ground, Batman wrestled the cane from his hands.

"I hear you like darkness," growled Batman. "So do I." He used his cape to envelop The Shade, wrapping him up until the villain passed out.

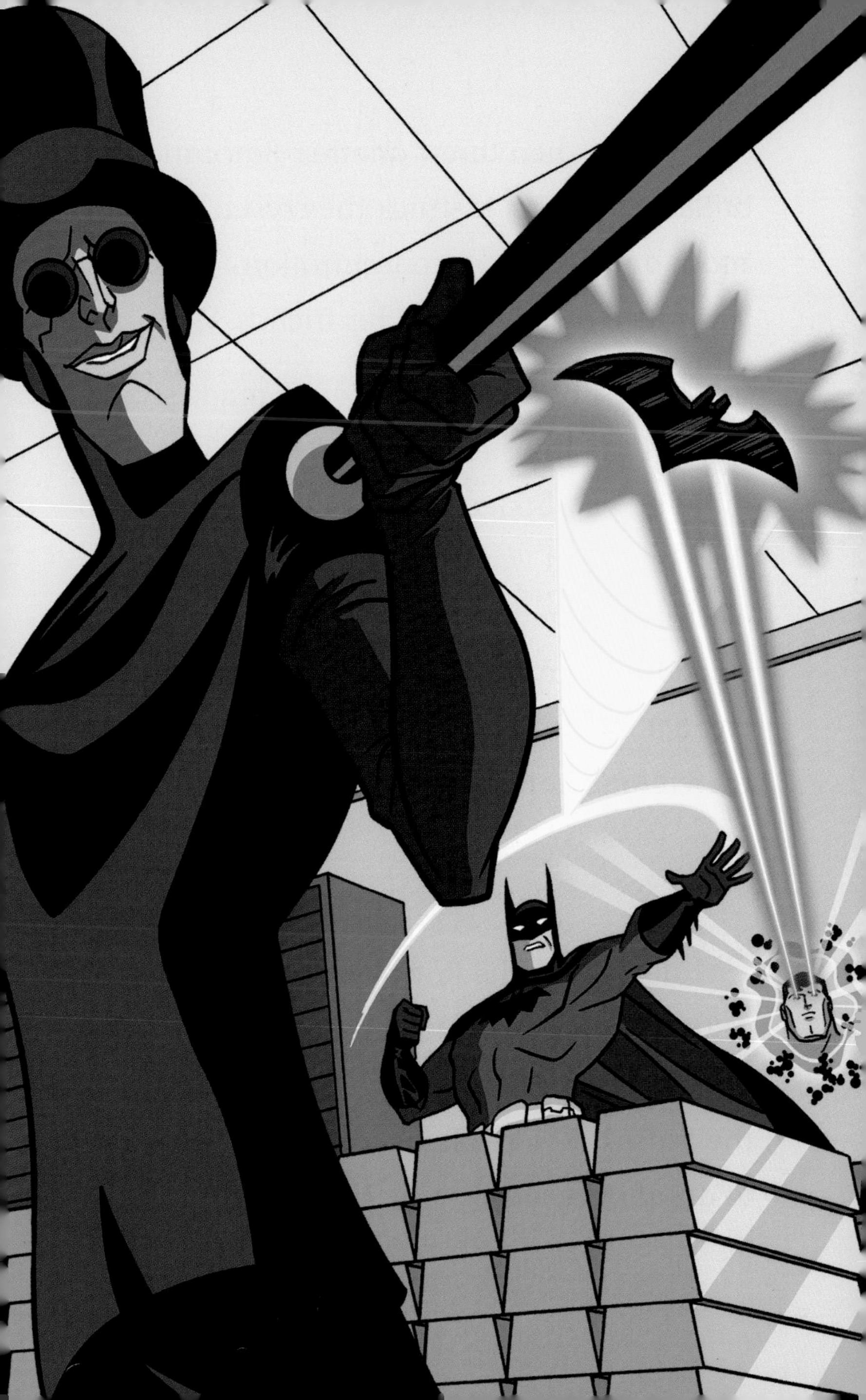

Batman then threw another Batarang at Star Sapphire. It struck the crystal in her mask and broke her concentration. The giant vise faded away, freeing his friends.

The rest of the Justice League made short work of the Injustice Gang. Tapping into the building's sprinkler system, Aquaman flooded the vault with water, and used his trident to electrify the puddle that the Injustice Gang stood in. Once knocked out, Green Lantern created a barred prison with his ring to hold the villains until the authorities arrived.

* * *

Later, inside the Batcave, Batman worked at the Batcomputer. Something had been bugging him ever since the failed robbery at the Federal Reserve Bank. He was now close to an answer.

"You wanted to see me?" asked a voice from above. Superman floated down to the cave floor to join his friend.

Batman held up his Batarang. "Notice anything odd about this?"

"Not really," said Superman, giving it a quick look.

"Look again," said Batman, turning the Batarang over. It now revealed two small holes burned into it. "Do those look familiar?"

"I'm not sure what you're getting at," stated Superman.

Batman pointed to the tiny holes. "This was the Batarang I threw at The Shade during the heist. I was trying to stop The Shade from using his cane. But then you shot my Batarang down. Why?"

"That's not possible," said Superman, taking the Batarang and turning it between his fingers. "I was with the rest of the Justice League, trapped in Star Sapphire's vise. We could barely keep it from crushing us."

"These are clearly burn marks from your laser vision," said Batman.

"And something else . . ." said the Man of Steel, his voice trailing off. He stared at the Batarang more intently with his X-ray vision. "Can you run it through your computer diagnostic again?"

Batman placed the Batarang into a slot on his computer to run a molecular scan. Superman was right. It was picking up something else.

"Tacheons," said Batman. "They are particles often left behind by time travel or time shifts."

"So maybe you weren't wrong. Maybe the lasers did come from me . . . another me from another time," said Superman. "It must've been for a good reason."

Batman placed the damaged Batarang into his security vault. It was a question to be answered some other time.

* * *

Inside Belle Reve Penitentiary, the lights flickered along the walls. The Shade, Cheetah, Ultra-Humanite, and Solomon Grundy were all getting used to their new surroundings. The sound of heavy heeled shoes pounded along the stone floor outside their cells.

CLOP! CLOP! CLOP!

Amanda Waller walked down the hallway when one of her prisoners called out to her.

"Thanks for the new roomies, Wally," said Harley Quinn, peeking her face out the window of her locked cell door. "But where's my puddin', Mista J? This is his gang of losers, isn't it?"

"The Joker's been sent back to Arkham Asylum. And his teammate, Star Sapphire, was taken to stand trial by the Green Lantern Corps," answered Waller. "Now shut your mouth, or I'll find a task that will keep you too busy to flap your trap."

Harley turned and quietly sulked to the back of her cell.

"All right, bring the new prisoner this way," commanded Waller.

The guards walked a man in orange attire down the hallway, past the cafeteria, to the far side of the building.

"We haven't had you back here for a while," said Waller with a smile. "But I'm sure you'll find the furnishings adequate. Although not to your usual high standards."

The cell door shut and the latch locked into place. The prisoner shuffled across his cramped cell and sat down on a dusty mattress. Boiling with anger, Lex Luthor rubbed his bald head as he pondered a sliver of light at his feet. He scowled when he traced the light's path to a thin window high up on the wall.

Even in this darkest of cells, light had found a way in.

(END)

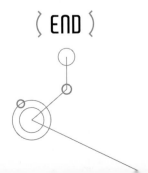

⟨ TARGET: APPREHENDED ⟩

THE SHADE

Richard Swift was a thief until he uncovered his connection to the Shadowlands — a dimension of darkness he was able to control. Tapping into his powers, he can create solid forms and objects out of shadows, control the darkness to his own desire, and summon and command demonic creatures from the Shadowlands. All of The Shade's dark powers can be channeled through his walking cane. It also has the ability to create smoke, project dark energy blasts, surround The Shade with a force field, and capture victims in a type of prison structure.

LEX LUTHOR

THE JOKER

CHEETAH

SINESTRO

CAPTAIN COLD

BLACK MANTA

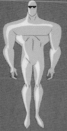

AMAZO

GORILLA GRODD

STAR SAPPHIRE

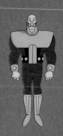

BRAINIAC

DARKSEID

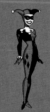

HARLEY QUINN

BIZARRO

THE SHADE

MONGUL

POISON IVY

MR. FREEZE

COPPERHEAD

ULTRA-
HUMANITE

CAPTAIN
BOOMERANG

SOLOMON GRUNDY

BLACK ADAM

DEADSHOT

CIRCE

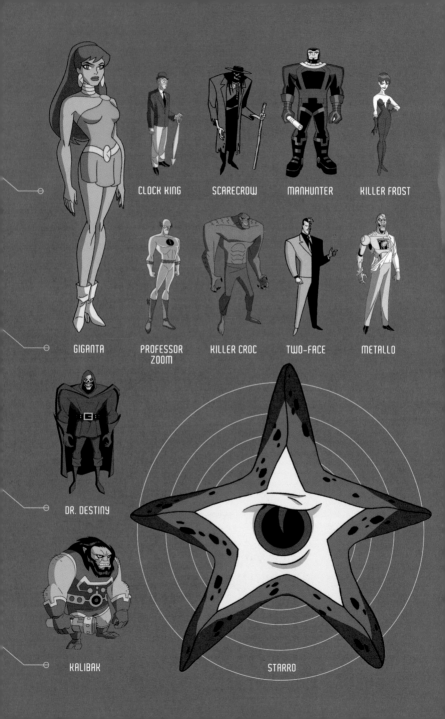

CLOCK KING

SCARECROW

MANHUNTER

KILLER FROST

GIGANTA

PROFESSOR ZOOM

KILLER CROC

TWO-FACE

METALLO

DR. DESTINY

KALIBAK

STARRO

STRENGTH IN NUMBERS

GLOSSARY

albino (al-BYE-noh)—a person or animal born without any natural coloring in the skin, hair, or eyes

barricade (BAR-rih-kade)—something set up to block passage into an area

cybernetic (SY-buhr-ne-tik)—something that is artificial and controlled by computers

duplicate (DOO-pluh-kit)—an exact copy

intellect (IN-tuh-lekt)—the power of the mind to think, reason, understand, and learn

ionized (EYE-uhn-eyezd)—changed into an ion, usually by removing one or more electrons from an atom or molecule

silhouette (sil-oo-ET)—an outline of something that shows its shape

technology (tek-NOL-uh-jee)—a piece of equipment or machinery developed with the use of scientific knowledge

transport (trans-PORT)—to move or carry something or someone from one place to another

unconscious (un-KON-shus)—not awake; not able to see, feel, or think

vise (VISSE)—a device with two jaws that open and close with a screw or lever

vortex (VOHR-tex)—air moving in a circular motion

THINK

1. The Justice League regroups at the Fortress of Solitude when the world goes dark. Where would you go first if our world was plunged into darkness?

2. Green Lantern creates a bulldozer with his power ring to control the prison inmates. What else could he have created to bring them under control?

3. The Justice League uses the Clock King's device to change the past. What event in history would you change if you had this device, and why?

WRITE

1. While the Justice League battles the shadow duplicates, the Injustice Gang gets away. Write a short chapter about what they do next.

2. Imagine if you had a secret base, like the Fortress of Solitude. Write a paragraph describing your base, where it is located, and what it would hold.

3. Lex Luthor scowls at a tiny window in his prison cell at the end of the story. Write short story in which that window plays a part in his escape.

AUTHOR

DEREK FRIDOLFS is the #1 *New York Times* bestselling writer of the DC Secret Hero Society series, and the Eisner nominated co-writer of *Batman Li'l Gotham*. He has worked in comics for more than 15 years as a writer, artist, and inker on such beloved properties as *Adventures of Superman*, *Detective Comics*, *Arkham City Endgame*, *Sensational Comics Featuring Wonder Woman*, *Justice League Beyond*, *Teen Titans Go*, *Scooby-Doo*, *Looney Tunes*, *Teenage Mutant Ninja Turtles*, *Dexter's Laboratory*, *Clarence*, *Regular Show*, and *Adventure Time*. He resides in California's central valley.

ILLUSTRATOR

TIM LEVINS is best known for his work on the Eisner Award-winning DC Comics series *Batman: Gotham Adventures*. Tim has illustrated other DC titles, such as *Justice League Adventures*, *Batgirl*, *Metal Men*, and *Scooby-Doo*, and has also done work for Marvel Comics and Archie Comics. Tim enjoys life in Midland, Ontario, Canada, with his wife, son, dog, and two horses.